Ladybird Readers

Sam and the Robots

T0322096

Series Editor: Sorrel Pitts
Text adapted by Coleen Degnan-Veness
Illustrated by Lisa Hunt
Song lyrics by Pippa Mayfield

LADYBIRD BOOKS

UK | USA | Canada | Ireland | Australia
India | New Zealand | South Africa

Ladybird Books is part of the Penguin Random House group of companies
whose addresses can be found at global.penguinrandomhouse.com.
www.penguin.co.uk   www.puffin.co.uk   www.ladybird.co.uk

Penguin
Random House
UK

First published 2016
Updated version reprinted 2024
007

Copyright © Ladybird Books Ltd, 2016, 2024

The moral rights of the author and illustrator have been asserted.

Printed in China

The authorized representative in the EEA is Penguin Random House Ireland,
Morrison Chambers, 32 Nassau Street, Dublin D02 YH68

A CIP catalogue record for this book is available from the British Library

ISBN: 978-0-241-25380-9

All correspondence to:
Ladybird Books
Penguin Random House Children's
One Embassy Gardens, 8 Viaduct Gardens, London SW11 7BW

MIX
Paper | Supporting
responsible forestry
FSC
www.fsc.org   FSC® C018179

Sam and
the Robots

Picture words

Sam

Pod

Dinner-Arms

Chock

Boots

robots

Sam was good at making things.

One day, he made a robot.

"I'm Pod," said the robot.
"Who are you?"

"I'm Sam," said Sam. "Pleased
to meet you."

Pod liked to make things, too.

"What shall we make now?" asked Sam one day.

"Can we make another robot, please?" said Pod.

So, Sam and Pod made a new robot. She was called Boots. Boots was a football robot and she was VERY good at her job. She got goal after goal after goal.

Sam's school won the next match, and the next one. They won ALL the football matches that year.

Sam and Pod made another new robot. He was called Dinner-Arms.

Dinner-Arms was a robot who cooked food at the school.

Dinner-Arms was VERY good at his job and made lots of lovely food for the children at school.

Sam and Pod made another robot called Chock. Chock was a robot who made excellent chocolates.

Everyone in the town wanted to eat Chock's lovely chocolates.

Sam and Pod were making more and more new robots.

Soon, the town was full of busy robots who were all working hard.

All day long, they washed and they cleaned, and they cleaned and they washed. The town was very clean. Everyone was happy because they didn't need to do any work.

But one day, something went wrong. The robots became too busy and they couldn't stop cleaning.

"Stop!" said Sam.

But the robots didn't stop. They cleaned and they washed and they cleaned.

Boots kicked ten goals . . . through ten windows at school!

"Stop, Boots!" shouted Sam.

But Boots didn't stop. She kicked the ball through five more windows!

All the children's plates were full,
but Dinner-Arms didn't stop cooking.

"Stop, Dinner-Arms!" cried Sam.

But Dinner-Arms didn't stop.
He cooked and he cooked and
soon the school was full of food.

Chock made strange chocolates. "Please stop, Chock!" cried Sam. "No one wants chocolate carrots or chocolate pencils!"

But Chock didn't stop. He made more and more of the strange chocolates. Soon, the town was full of chocolates.

Pod, too, started to do strange things.

"I know what's wrong," said Sam. "You robots need a holiday!"

"What's a holiday?" asked Pod.

"On a holiday, you have time to rest and have fun," said Sam.

"Yes please," said Pod. "But we'll want to work, too . . ."

So, Sam and the robots got on a train to the beach.

"The train is fun—but we still want to work," said Pod.

The robots started to work. They washed and they cleaned until the train was very clean.

Soon, the train arrived at the beach. "Now we can rest and have some fun," said Sam.

"The beach looks really fun!" said Pod. "All that sand needs cleaning! And there's lots of water to help us!"

The robots started to clean and wash. But the beach was very big and there was too much sand. They couldn't make it clean.

"No! Robots, please stop!" cried
Sam. "You mustn't work on holiday!
You should rest on the beach,
like this."

Sam lay down to rest. Then all
the robots lay down, too.

But soon all the robots were bored and they all got up again.

"Robots don't like resting," said Pod. "We're bored. We need to be busy."

Then Sam had an idea. "I know what we can do," he said.

Sam, Pod and all the other robots were very busy. They worked hard together and they used the sand to make a big building.

Sam and the robots made a big sandcastle. They made that sandcastle all day long and the sandcastle got bigger and bigger and bigger!

"We've made a good sandcastle!" said the robots in the end.

"No," said Sam, "you've made a GREAT sandcastle!"

Then Sam said, "Now, we'll all eat ice cream."

"What's ice cream?" asked Pod.

"It's a lovely, cold food," said Sam.

"No, we're thirsty. We need a lovely, cold drink, please," said Pod.

"Yes please, a lovely, cold drink," said all the robots.

Sam and the robots got the last train back home from the beach.

"It was a great holiday," said Pod, "but I'm happy because we're going home."

"And we're VERY happy because we're going back to work!" said the other robots.

Activities

The key below describes the skills practiced in each activity.

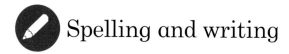 Spelling and writing

📖 Reading

💬 Speaking

🎧 Listening*

❓ Critical thinking

🎵 Singing*

✳ Preparation for the Cambridge Young Learners exams

1 Match the words to the pictures.

1 Sam

2 Pod

3 Dinner-Arms

4 Chock

5 Boots

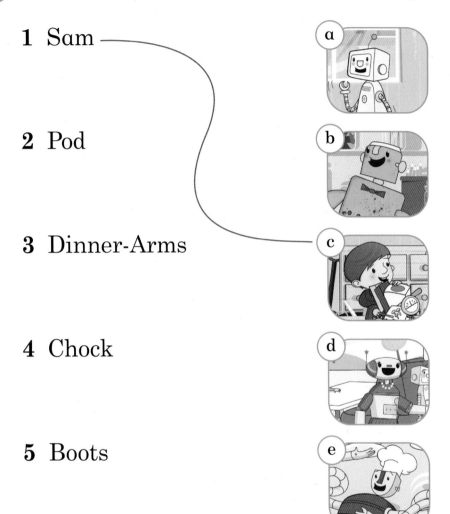

2 **Look at the letters.**
Write the words. 📖 ✏️

(b o s o t r)

1 Sam was good at making ....robots.....

(s a h l l)

2 "What .... we make now?"
asked Sam one day.

(r n a o t e h)

3 "Can we make .... robot,
please?" said Pod.

(l b f o a o l t)

4 Boots was a .... robot.

(l o a g)

5 Boots could get one ....
after another.

3 Read the story.
Choose the right words and write
them on the lines. 📖 ✏️ ✦

1	where	who	when
2	play	played	playing
3	other	another	some
4	lots	lot	many

Sam and Pod made a new robot

[1] _____who_____ they called Boots.

She was very good at [2] _____

football. Then, Sam and Pod made

[3] _____ robot called Dinner-Arms.

He made [4] _____ of lovely food for

the children at school.

4 Talk about the two pictures with a friend. How are they different?

In picture a, Sam is standing, but in picture b, he is walking.

5 Do the crossword.

Down

1 A game that is played in many countries of the world.

4 The place where many children go every day and play football.

Across

2 When you kick the football, you want to get this.

3 Football games are called this.

5 Sam and Pod like to . . . things.

6 Ask and answer the questions with a friend. 💬 ❓

1 *Which robot plays football?*

Boots.

2 What is she doing?

3 Where is the football match?

4 Who is watching the football match, do you think?

7 **Look and read. Write the answers as complete sentences.**

1 Where did Dinner-Arms work?

He worked in Sam's school.

2 What was Dinner-Arms good at?

....

3 How many plates of food can you see?

....

8 **Read the story. Write some words to complete the sentences.**

> Soon, the town was full of busy robots who were all working hard. All day long, they cleaned and they washed. The town was very clean. Everyone was happy because they didn't need to do any work.

1 There were lots of ___busy robots___ in the town.

2 They were working hard all

_____.

3 No one needed to _____.

9 Look and read. Choose the correct words and write them on the lines.

> strange   match   robot   goals

1 We can use this word to describe people and things that aren't normal. ...strange...

2 This can work like a person and it looks like a person, too. ....

3 Footballers win the match when they get lots of these. ....

4 This is the word for a football game. ....

10 **Circle the correct words.**

1 But one day, something went
right. / wrong.

2 The robots couldn't **start / stop**
cleaning.

3 Boots kicked the ball through the
school **windows. / doors.**

4 Dinner-Arms cooked and cooked
and soon the school was **full /
empty** of food.

5 Then, Chock made lots and lots of
lovely / strange chocolates.

11 Write *got on*, *look at*, or *sat down*.

1 Sam and the robots .... got on .... a train to the beach.

2 As soon as the robots .... the train, they started cleaning.

3 Pod .... next to Sam.

4 Chock .... opposite Sam.

5 The robots didn't stop cleaning. They didn't .... the countryside out of their windows.

12 Write the correct form of the verbs. 📖 ✏️

"You should ......<u>rest</u>...... **(rest)** on the beach," said Sam. All the robots .... **(lie)** down. But soon they all .... **(get up)** again. "We .... **(be)** bored," said Pod. "We .... **(need)** to be busy." Then, Sam .... **(have)** an idea.

13 Order the story. Write 1—5.

_____ Sam and the robots used the sand to make a big building.

_____ Sam had an ice cream and the robots had a lovely, cold drink.

__1__ Sam decided to go on holiday.

_____ Sam and the robots got the last train back home.

_____ The robots were bored and didn't want to lie down on the beach.

14 **Look at the pictures.**
Tell the story to your friend.

1

2

3

4

5

6

The robots arrived at the beach . . .

15 **Listen, and ✓ the boxes.** 🎧 ✦

1 What did everyone want?

a

b ✓

c

2 What has the robot made?

a

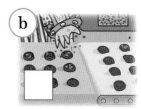
b

c

3 What food is it?

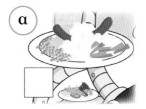
a

b

c

4 Where are they going?

a

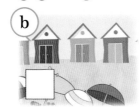
b

c

16 **Ask and answer the questions with a friend.** ⬤ ⬤

1

> *Would you like to go on holiday?*

> *Yes, I would.*

2 Where do you go on holiday?

3 How do you travel there?

4 What do you like doing on holiday?

17 Sing the song. 🎵

All Sam's robots were good at different jobs,
But one day the robots couldn't stop.
All the robots washed and cleaned.
They cleaned and they washed, and the town was clean.

Sam told his robots, "You all need a holiday!
Let's get on a train and have some fun."
But all the robots washed and cleaned.
They cleaned and washed, and the train was clean.

Sam told his robots, "Look! Here's the beach!
Let's have a rest and have some fun."
But all the robots started to clean.
The beach was very big—too much sand to clean!

Sam told his robots, "You mustn't work on holiday.
Let's have a rest and enjoy the sun."
But all the robots got up and said,
"We're bored when we don't have anything to clean!"

Sam told his robots, "I've got an idea!
Let's make a sandcastle here on the beach."
All the robots started to help, and they made
a great sandcastle there on the beach.

Sam told his robots about ice cream,
But they wanted a drink, not ice cream.
They all went home and the robots said,
"What a great holiday, but now we can clean!"

Visit **www.ladybirdeducation.co.uk**

for more FREE Ladybird Readers resources

✓ Digital edition
  of every title
✓ Audio tracks (US/UK)
✓ Answer keys
✓ Lesson plans

✓ Role-plays
✓ Classroom
  display material
✓ Flashcards
✓ User guides

Register and sign up to the newsletter to receive your
FREE classroom resource pack!